D0116658

For my kindergarten friends
—J. E.

For Irene and Alex
for being as fabulous as a pair of frog boots!
—J. H.

STERLING CHILDREN'S BOOKS
New York

An Imprint of Sterling Publishing Co., Inc.
1166 Avenue of the Americas
New York, NY 10036

STERLING CHILDREN'S BOOKS and the distinctive Sterling Children's Books logo
are registered trademarks of Sterling Publishing Co., Inc.

Text © 2019 Jill Esbaum
Illustrations © 2019 Joshua Heinsz

All rights reserved. No part of this publication may be reproduced,
stored in a retrieval system, or transmitted in any form or by any means
(including electronic, mechanical, photocopying, recording, or otherwise)
without prior written permission from the publisher.

ISBN 978-1-4549-3297-0

Distributed in Canada by Sterling Publishing
c/o Canadian Manda Group, 664 Annette Street
Toronto, Ontario M6S 2C8, Canada
Distributed in the United Kingdom by GMC Distribution Services
Castle Place, 166 High Street, Lewes, East Sussex BN7 1XU, England
Distributed in Australia by NewSouth Books,
University of New South Wales, Sydney, NSW, 2052, Australia

For information about custom editions, special sales, and premium
and corporate purchases, please contact Sterling Special Sales
at 800-805-5489 or specialsales@sterlingpublishing.com.

Manufactured in Malaysia
Lot #:
2 4 6 8 10 9 7 5 3 1
12/19

sterlingpublishing.com

Interior and cover design by Irene Vandervoort

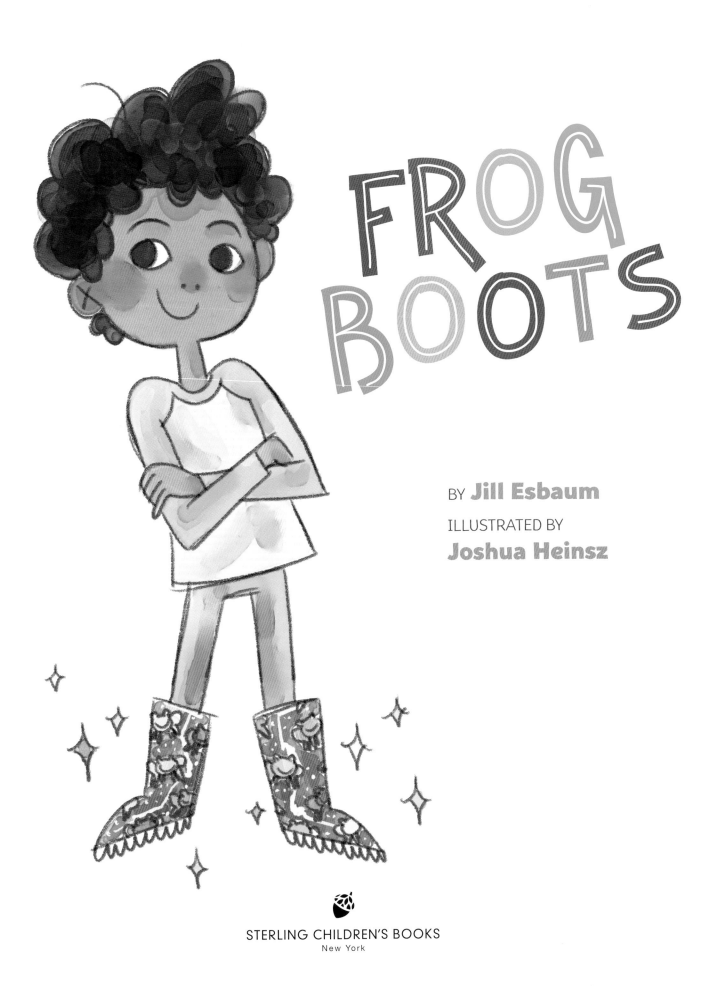

FROG BOOTS

BY **Jill Esbaum**

ILLUSTRATED BY
Joshua Heinsz

STERLING CHILDREN'S BOOKS
New York

Dylan didn't want to start a new school with the same old stuff. One cool thing, that's all he needed. But Mom wouldn't buy *anything* he liked.

Not the ginormous backpack.

Not the camo underwear.

Not the scratch-and-gag stickers.

He dragged his feet along like bricks.
Until . . .

"Mom, WAIT. Poison dart frogs. I love poison dart frogs!"

"These?" she said. "Not *those*, with the dump trucks? Because these shimmery ones . . . I'm not even sure they're—"

"C'mon, Mom. *Pleeeease*? I won't ask for one more thing!"

Dylan *clomp-tromped* from the store feeling cool and smart. Taller, even.

He loved the boots so much he wore them to bed. Which is how he discovered that the *green* frogs . . .

. . . glowed in the dark!

Who'd ever had such **AWESOME** boots?

Nobody, that's who!

Kids were going to think the boots— and Dylan—were super cool.

On his first day at Madison, Dylan raced to Circle Time, *clomp-tromp, clomp-tromp* . . .

. . . and stuck his feet right out into the middle.

It worked, too. Everybody was looking. Dylan was about to reveal the secret of the green frogs when a kid said, "Ms. Kory, that boy's wearing girl boots."

Dylan bristled. "These aren't girl boots!"

"Are too," said a ponytailed girl. "They're *purple*. My little sister has those."

Everybody laughed and laughed.

Ms. Kory banged a tambourine for quiet.

"Feet in the middle, please."

While she got kids talking about Same and Different, Dylan slowly pulled back his feet, feeling sweaty and prickly and dumb.

And very, very small.

"How was your first day at Madison?" Mom asked.
"Okay," said Dylan, *clomp-tromping* to his room.
Tell his mom that the boots he'd begged for turned out
to be girl boots? No way!

There. The dopey things could rot, for all he cared.

Dylan devised a plan to avoid more embarrassment at his new school. For the rest of the week, he simply wouldn't look at anybody.

That turned out to be quite a challenge.

But he managed it.

Friday night, Dylan paged through his favorite book. He still loved poison dart frogs. It wasn't their fault they got stuck being on girl boots.

He knew the words by heart. "Some of these poisonous pipsqueaks are only one inch long."

That made him wonder. . . .

He found his ruler.

One inch. But something was different.
Whoa. No glow!
Dylan tried to forget about the greenies.

But the faded little guys
hopped right into his dreams.

The next morning Dylan moved the boots to his windowsill.
"There. A little sunshine will fix you right up."

Then he yanked the curtains shut. Just because he felt sorry for the frogs didn't mean he wanted to be reminded that he owned girl boots.

After dark, though, Dylan had to peek. Instantly, he remembered...

How the greenies had surprised him that first night.

How he'd thought the boots were *awesome*.

How they made him feel cool and smart. Taller, even.

Until they didn't.

Still. To never wear them again?

Maybe he could just wear them on weekends. Who would know?

Yes! The boots were perfect
for the mud hole out back.

SPLOOSH,
      SPLUNK,
            SPLOOSH

And for getting super close
to the ducklings in the park.
    "Mom, I can't even feel
the rocks!"

It was especially fun reading *about* poison dart frogs *to* poison dart frogs.

" . . . and look, here's where you live. The rainforest!"

Dylan wore the boots to bed. They felt so good on his feet. So right-where-they-belonged.

He wiggled his toes. These boots and those dump truck boots were probably exactly the same inside. Why, then, were these girl boots? Because they were purple?

"Phooey," he said. "Girls don't *own* purple!"

When Dylan *clomp-tromped* into his classroom the next morning, he caught a boy named Jeremiah staring at the boots.

Dylan looked down . . . but only to remind himself how much he loved his boots.

His feel-so-right boots.
His I-don't-care-if-they're-purple boots.

Then he looked up, looked Jeremiah right in the eyes.

"Poison dart frogs," he said bravely. "Actual size."

"Amazing," said Jeremiah. "Wish I had those."

The ponytailed girl overheard. "But they're *girl* boots!"

"Not when they're on boy feet," Dylan said.

Jeremiah laughed and laughed.

Suddenly, Dylan felt cool and smart. Taller, even.

Awesome.